CREATE A STORY

THE INVASION OF THE VIKINGS

**Concept and Text by
ANDREW MASSINGHAM**

**Illustrations by
ALEXANDR NIKIFOROV**

AUSTIN MACAULEY PUBLISHERS™
LONDON • CAMBRIDGE • NEW YORK • SHARJAH

BACKGROUND INFORMATION

Hello explorer! Before you begin your journey, please take a few minutes to read through the information provided below. It is very important that you know a bit about the harsh, dangerous times you are about to enter.

If you don't understand a word, underline it!

The History

Many years ago, in the year 793 AD, Britain was invaded by... THE VIKINGS! They travelled over from Scandinavia in search of rich, fertile land to raise their animals and grow their crops. After all, British land was extremely valuable, making those who owned it very rich. They first invaded the north, attacking the Saxon settlements, killing its people and taking their land. Many battles were fought and lost by the many kings of Britain.

Your story takes place as the Vikings travel down south to Wessex. The Vikings are growing in power and there seems to be no hope for the native Saxon people...

Secondary Research

It is recommended that you take some time to carry out research on the Vikings invasion. Understanding the setting for your story is very important in order for you to write an accurate, detailed short story.

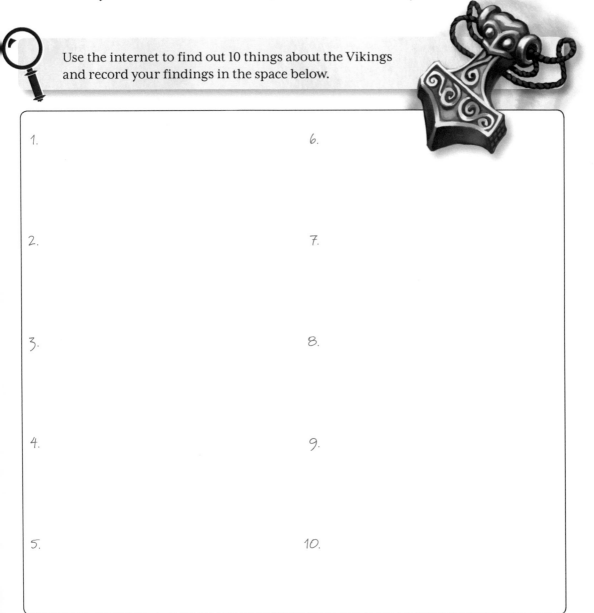

Use the internet to find out 10 things about the Vikings and record your findings in the space below.

1.

2.

3.

4.

5.

6.

7.

8.

9.

10.

THE BEGINNING

Embark To begin a journey.

You are about to embark on a journey through the early Middle Ages of Britain. You must first choose a main character who has the ability to defeat the Viking enemy and reclaim the people's land. Think about what personality traits this main character will need to have to be successful on their quest. Think about what emotions will drive them to continue on their journey however difficult it may become. Think about what items will allow them to perform to the best of their ability. Please choose carefully. The people look to you to save their country.

The Plotline

? You should now choose the main focus of your story. What adventure are you going to embark on?

○ **The Farmer**

You are a skilled farmer who has been asked to go and help the Viking enemy farm their land as they prepare for a harsh winter. Secretly, though, your main goal is to find out valuable information about the enemy.

○ **The King**

Your kingdom is attacked, so you flee to isolated swamplands. You must go to the Vikings and negotiate a deal so the fighting stops.

Betrayed To hurt someone by doing something morally wrong or by going against them.

○ **The Princess**

Your father, the king of Northumbria, is betrayed and killed by his most trusted nobleman. The nobleman wants to steal your father's buried silver - it's your job to find and protect it!

Nobleman A man in history who was rich and had a high position in society.

Personalise your protagonist

Protagonist the leading actor in your story

Next, describe your character's personality. Place a tick next to two of these traits:

- Brave
- Loyal

- Kind
- Greedy

- Sensitive
- Protective

Your character's emotions: think about your character - how would they feel during the story you have picked? Place a tick next to two of the words.

- Anger
- Pride

- Sadness
- Happiness

- Hope
- Trust

Choose one skill and one fear which your main character has. Think of how you can use the skill to your advantage in defeating the Vikings. Plan out a way you could overcome your fear if you are faced by it on your journey.

Skill
- A beautiful singer
- A very talented fisher
- An excellent navigator of the land

Fears
- The dark
- Loud noises
- Confined spaces

What is the name of your character?

The Trusted Pet

Gratitude being thankful for an act of kindness

You are now almost ready to begin this exciting but dangerous journey. Your people want to offer you a trusted pet as a token of their <u>gratitude</u>. The trusted pet will act as your side-kick who will be able to help you achieve the overall mission. Choose carefully. A trusted side-kick must be able to support you in the most dangerous and important circumstances.

 Choose one pet who will join you along the way.

○ **Meet Rohan**
The Reliable Raven

Rohan is a veteran serviceman who was awarded the 'Gold Star', for successfully revealing the enemy's exact location in a past battle.

○ **Meet Henry**
The Hardworking Horse

Now, Henry might not be the most intelligent horse in the world, but he works harder than any other. If you want to get somewhere quickly, then Henry is the pet for you!

Persuasive To be able to cause people to do or believe something.

○ **Meet Pamela**
The <u>Persuasive</u> Pig

Pamela is a powerful businesswoman who runs the most successful farm in the whole of Britain. If you want to negotiate a deal with the Viking enemy, you need Pamela by your side.

Let's get your bag packed!

 You have a long journey ahead of you so you must pack only the essentials. You have enough room to take three out of the six items below with you. Choose carefully. These items will come in very handy along the road. Pick three items:

○ 1. A bone flute

○ 2. A lamp

○ 3. Drinking water

○ 5. A map

○ 4. A spare pair of boots

○ 6. Your sword

What were the Vikings like?

The Vikings weren't afraid to die in battle as they believed they would go to 'Valhalla', the afterlife for brave fallen warriors.

Vikings absolutely loved fish!

The Vikings loved riddles, stories and songs.

The Vikings were famously known for navigating the sea. They would be able to mark their location and track their journey through observing the positions and activity of the sun, stars and birds.

The Viking's built boats that could travel up to 200 miles a day!

Vikings were known for their excellent hygiene.

A Vikings most prized possession is their sword which would have been handed down to them by their mother and father.

Hygiene the practice of keeping yourself clean.

LEARNING ACTIVITY

In your story, you should include examples of the following grammar. This will help to make your story more exciting for your reader!

Adverb

An adverb explains the action which is being described.

Example the horse galloped quickly.

Adjective

An adjective describes a person, place or thing.

Example She was a large, fearless woman.

Use the space below to think of your own adverbs and adjectives for your story.

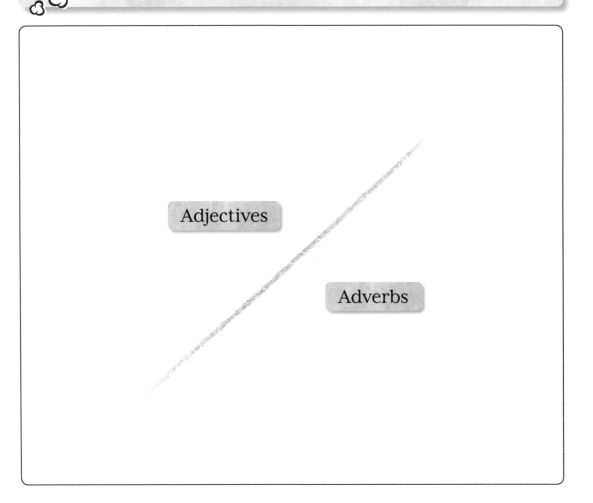

Adjectives

Adverbs

THE MIDDLE

It is now time to plan the middle of your story. Here, your main character will be confronted with a problem, and will face a conflict which they will have to overcome. In your story, you should include adverbs and adjectives.

Conflict A strong disagreement between people.

The Problem & Conflict

Choose one problem that your main character will face on their adventure. How will they overcome it?

- There is an outbreak of very bad weather.

- You are captured and enslaved by the Viking enemy.

- You get lost. **Outbreak** The sudden start of something.

Now choose someone who you will be in conflict with from the options below.

○ **The Sorceress**

Aim Seeks revenge on the Saxon people for banishing her as a child for accidental sorcery.

○ **The Viking**

Aim To be feared by the Saxons. In battle he displays great strength and loyalty to his people.

○ **The Priest**

Aim To stop you from going on your mission as he senses grave danger.

Sorceress A person who has magical powers.

THE END

Plot Twist

A **plot twist** is an unexpected turn of events. It is used to keep the story interesting and the reader unsure of what will happen next.

Think of your own plot twist that will surprise your readers.

The Climax & Aftermath

It is now time for the main event to take place in your story. What are you going to do to achieve your overall mission and resolve your conflicts?

Make sure that you tell the reader what happens to your characters after the main event is over.

Your main character is...

Your trusted pet is...

Your conflicting character is...

Let's get drawing!

Build your own self-sufficient Anglo-Saxon village

In order to survive, the Anglo-Saxon people had to become self-sufficient. This meant using what was available to them so they could eat, drink and carry out their daily activities. Follow the instructions below which will support you in building your village.

Use the images below as a guide for what is needed in a self-sufficient village.

 An Anglo-Saxon home. Your village requires wooden, thatched homes for the people to live in. Draw 3 houses in the middle of your village.

 Space for your livestock. In front of your houses, draw a fenced area for your animals to be kept in.

 Pigs. Draw two pigs in the fenced area in front of your houses.

Livestock farm animals

 Sheep. Make sure to include some sheep in your Anglo-Saxon village. Allow some space on the edge of the village where they will be able to graze.

 An Oxen and Plough. Draw a small square on the edge of the village. This space will be used to plough the fields in order to make them ready to plant seeds on.

Graze eat grass in a field

Plough a large farming tool used to cut lines in the soil ready for planting seeds

Lastly, look at your surroundings. Name two essential things that you will need to get from the body of water nearby?

Think about the wooded area behind the village. Name two things which you can make from using the wood's natural resources.

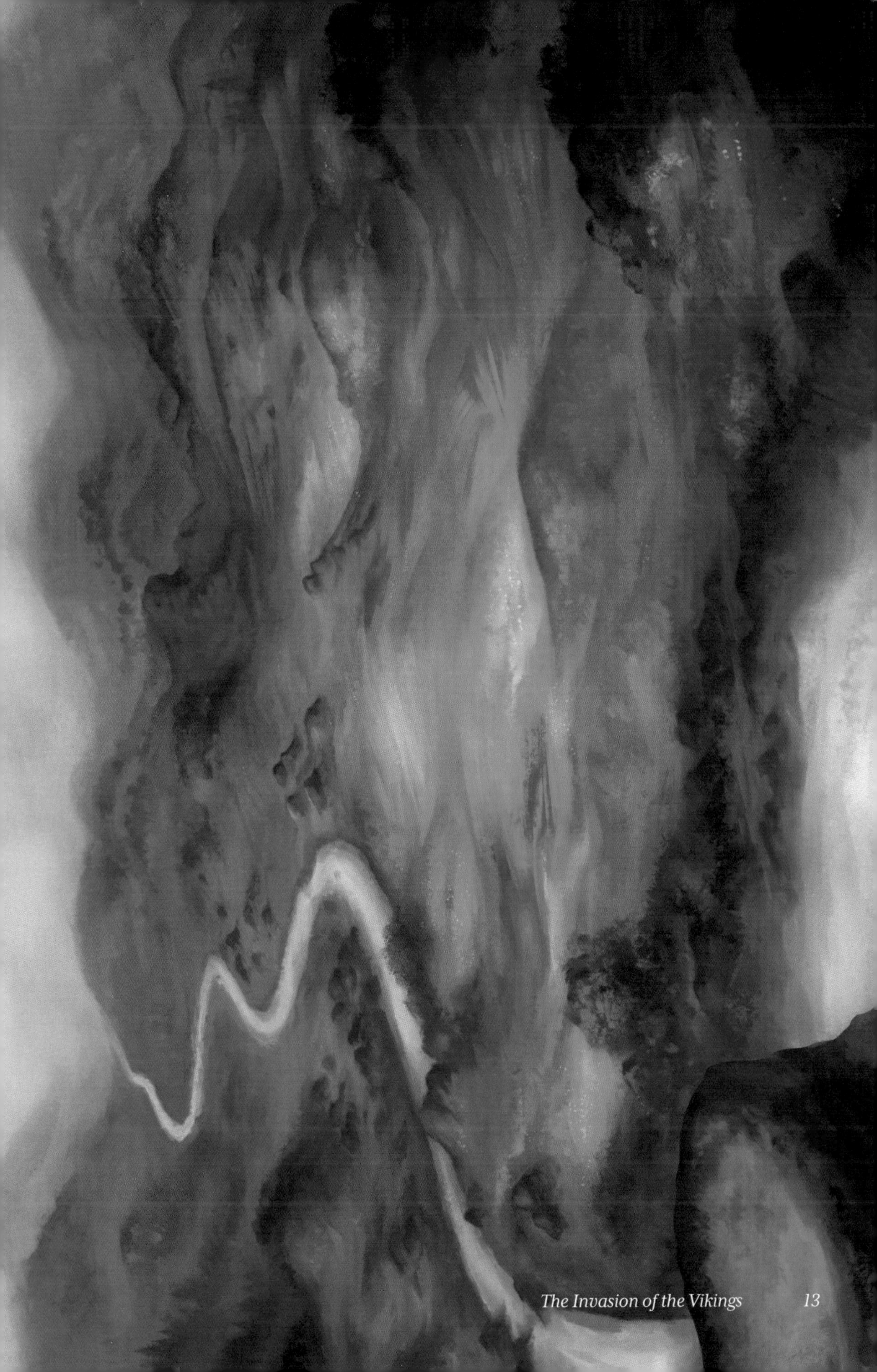

YOUR STORYBOARD

Use the boxes below to plan out how your story's events will unfold through the use of graphic illustrations. Describe what is happening in the lines below.

1

2

_____

_____

3

4

_____

_____

5

6

7

8

First Draft

You are now ready to write your short story... Follow the plan you have just worked through, and, most importantly, enjoy yourself!

Unlock that brilliant mind of yours, and write your first imaginative adventure!

SELF-REFLECTION & IMPROVEMENTS

It is always very important to self-reflect in order to improve your work. Self-reflection is about asking yourself questions which will give you a better understanding of your writing habits and decision making.

What was your favourite part of the story and why?

How will you improve your story?

How would you change your main character to benefit the mission?

Time to get a second opinion. Ask your parent or a teacher to give you some feedback on your story.

Read your self-reflection and the comments from the parent/teacher. What will you do to improve the story you have written?

FINAL DRAFT

Use the notes from the self-reflection and the improvements to make your story even better. Take your time and have fun. We are all looking forward to reading your first fantastic short story

VISUALISATION EXERCISE

My favourite scene

Now that you have written an excellent short story, it is time to draw a sketch of your favourite scene from your story. We want you as a writer to remember your work, and what better way than to close your eyes and imagine.

Write down at least five things that you can see in your imagination.

Once you can visualise your surroundings, pick up a pencil and sketch what you see. Imagine you are drawing a picture of what you see in front of you.

Visualise To form a picture of someone or something in your mind.

This box too small for your drawing? Use another piece of paper.

WHERE NEXT?

Emotional intelligence
The ability to be aware
of, control and express
one's emotions

Kindness being caring
and considerate towards
someone or something.

Relate to your protagonist

You have now written an excellent short story, but it is very important that you are always looking to improve your writing. This exercise will improve your emotional intelligence which will allow you to better connect with your future protagonists. As an author, it is very important that you fully engage with the characters in the stories you write. Let's take a look at kindness.

When did your main character show kindness? Who or what was it to? How did it make your main character feel?

Write down two occasions where you have shown kindness to someone or something?

How did it make you feel?

How did it make the people around you feel?

THE FINAL TOUCHES

Writer's Tick List

Use this to make sure you've got all the elements for your Viking adventure!

☐ I personalised my main character

☐ I made use of my three chosen items

☐ I included a trusted pet that helped me achieve my mission

☐ I included one adjective and one adverb in my story

☐ I overcame a problem and conflict in my story

☐ I used visual graphics when planning my story to give my story further structure

☐ I learnt about what was needed to survive in an Anglo-Saxon village

☐ Through self-reflection and feedback, I improved my story in its final draft

Book signing

When a book does well, authors will often do book signings. This is where the author puts their signature on a copy of their book for a fan.

Why not take a chance to practice signing your story in the space below?

Illustrations by Alexandr Nikiforov
Design by Tom Castle

A CIP catalogue record for this title is available from the British Library.

ISBN 978-1-52891-571-7 (paperback)
ISBN 978-1-52891-572-4 (Kindle eBook)
ISBN 978-1-52896-135-6 (ePub eBook)

www.austinmacauley.com

First Published (2019)

Austin Macauley Publishers Ltd.
25 Canada Square
Canary Wharf
London
E14 5LQ